Say Hello to the Animals!

Say Hello to the Animals!

Ian Whybrow

Tim Warnes

MACMILLAN CHILDREN'S BOOKS

Cock-a-doodle-doo!

Ready, steady, off we go.
Round the farm to say hello.

Who's that nibbling, half asleep?
Say hello to the dozy sheep.

Hello, Sheep!
Baaa, baaa, baaa!

Here's the sty – not very big –
Say hello to the little pink pig.

Hello, Pig!

Oink, oink, oink!

Who's on the fence beside her pen?
Say hello to the speckly hen.

Hello, Hen!
Cluck, cluck, cluck!

Look who's hiding under those sticks.
Say hello to the fluffy chicks.

Hello, Chicks!
Cheep, cheep, cheep!

Look in the barn – who's in here now?
Say hello to the friendly cow.

Hello, Cow!
Moo, moo, moo!

Who's that paddling in the muck?
Say hello to the splashy duck.

Hello, Duck!
Quack, quack, quack!

Who's in the *stable*? Yes, of course!
Say hello to the hungry horse.

Hello, Horse!
Neigh, neigh, neigh!

"Are you ready, Ella Rose? Off you go with your Hellos!"
With a Hello and a big whiskery kiss from You-know-who. – I.W.

For Nick, Anna, Fraser and Alex:
"Hello you Lows!" – T.W.

First published 2005 by Macmillan Children's Books
This edition published 2006 by Macmillan Children's Books
a division of Macmillan Publishers Limited
20 New Wharf Road, London N1 9RR
Basingstoke and Oxford
Associated companies throughout the world
www.panmacmillan.com

ISBN : 978-1-4050-2160-9

7 9 8 6

A CIP catalogue record for this book is available from the British Library.

Printed in China